World Fraternity?

World Fraternity?

A BOOMER'S DREAM

a novelette

NENÉ LA ROSA

World Fraternity? A Boomer's Dream

Published by Wheatmark™
610 East Delano Street, Suite 104
Tucson, Arizona 85705 U.S.A.
www.wheatmark.com

International Standard Book Number: 978-1-58736-915-5
Library of Congress Control Number: 2007932385

*To the soldiers fallen
in Vietnam*

*Avant d'etre Francais,
je suis homme.*

—Montesquieu

Chapter I

Dear Dad:

I am sending you this synopsis of my life from Canada, my country and home now, hoping that you will read it rather than throwing it in the wastebasket like all my letters before this. If we had been close, I'd have confided in you and you'd have known me as a father knows his son. You'd have known the depth of my being, my aspirations, hopes and dreams and we wouldn't be total strangers. As things were and are, you still have to guess who I am inside. Lack of communication, of course, has made us two human beings with little in common.

You are a son of Mars and I of Apollo. You have the genes of a warrior with the instinct to subjugate others by force, while. I love peace and believe in convincing others with the power of argument in an amicable debate. You like the roar of the victors in stadiums and arenas, while I love the silence of libraries and museums. While I am a smaller spitting image of you in body, probably a further source of your unhappiness with me, I inherited a tendency toward my mother's character. Although I do not have a body as large as yours and its stamina, I've still defended my rights. I've had a lot of failures trying to reach my goals, falling down many times, but I have always gotten right up and kept going toward them. I reached some and many are out there yet, but I am always in a march toward them.

Will I ever reach all of them? I don't know. If they are still worth pursuing I will pursue them for the rest of my life and at any cost. At any rate, my failures have made me a little wiser. I've seen so many clay idols, that I had adored, fall into smithereens, while small facts have taken the shape of solid rocks on which my life now stands. While you were away bombing North Korea, while I was a very small child, mom was the only company for me and I for her. I remember when I was old enough to see up there how handsome you looked to me in your air force pilot's uniform in the picture standing on the fireplace mantel in the living room! After the truce, we still didn't see much of you. Perhaps your job as a TWA pilot kept you away from home most of the time, not counting your Reserve duty, the time you spent at the American Legion Post 203, your participation in every Republican party rally and campaign.

You are a born Leader, dad, in every way. I remember the vehemence of your speeches against the enemy, so contrasting with the humble speechless devotion you showed at the mention of our country or at the sight of our glorious flag. Yet someone was circulating rumors that you were being faithful to our country but not to my mother. You were philandering, and also kept a steady mistress. I don't know if mom ever believed them, but I caught her crying now and then. You see, dear dad, I always had my mother around me, but you were never near me or her. And she was beautiful then! She was tall and fair, with her light brown hair, her soft speech, but with words of wisdom. My mother, bless her memory, told me that at my birth you made a wish to see me as a captain of a warship when I grew up. I did disappoint you in this.

I remember in one of our few times together that at the news of the fall of Dien Bien Phu, you said, "The French haven't had a war genius since the days of Napoleon." They had been taking a beating in Vietnam because of their inept generals, so they sent their famous general Salan to save the day. The French troops were dirty and fatigued by years of fighting in the jungle there. What they saw was Salan, coming to lead them in wearing a plumed helmet, white uniform, and riding a white stallion, as if he was presiding in a military parade on the Champs Elysees! You, dear dad, commented to us: "You don't win wars with feathered helmets and white uniforms! It takes good soldiers and good weapons! We have what it takes to stop the Commies there. Now that China's Red, we Americans have a duty to challenge the domino effect and not let Vietnam become ' Red.' " President Lyndon B. Johnson and many others , like minded as you, were ready to stop the Red expansion and fight there where the French had failed. That's how the Vietnam War started. It cost 50 thousand of our valiant young men and who knows how many lives of Vietnamese.

In 1967 when I was almost seventeen years old and would soon reach draft age, you dear dad, were so glad there was a war going on and you told me how you dreamed of see me fighting in Vietnam and covering myself with glory. Had you considered Aristotle, who said that people have the kind of government they deserve. Did you read that? Even if the Vietnamese people chose to experience the hardships of life under a communist regime, why didn't we let them be free to suffer it and then act themselves to change it. They'd find out that our way of life and our form of government are a better choice. In time they would undoubtedly want to have our way of life and our form of government, and fight for it to happen. You, dear dad, thought that I was a child with foolish thoughts. Anyway, we went to war.

Do you remember that ever since my first elementary school days I'd been good friends with Mary Lou Anderson? She was a beautiful girl and always kind and smiling then and when she and I were high school seniors she had a boyfriend, Tom Carson. Remember him? He was a little older than I am, and he was already fighting in Vietnam in 1967. When Tom was drafted I kept telling Mary Lou that her boyfriend probably would be sent to Germany, or better yet, that peace would be restored before long and nobody would have to fight anywhere. Unfortunately Tom was sent to Vietnam. In two months he came back home to us in a flag-draped pine box. Tom's death left Mary Lou's life in complete turmoil, as you know from the newspapers. Tom was a solid but gentle guy with dark brown intelligent eyes. I had talked with him in a serious way a few times. His father owned the small nursery on Main Street. Tom hoped to some day run his father's business and expand and modernize it. He confided that as soon things were ripe, he'd planned to ask Mary Lou to marry him.

Tom was one of those individuals who by nature easily acquiesce and adapt to the circumstances they find themselves in. There no perpetual agitation within him searching for solutions to the besetting problems of the individual and society. No burning ideals consumed his life. His clear goals were set near and within definable means and limits. The distant echo of human suffering didn't exactly reach him. His quiet, prosaic way made him a milestone of reference to Mary Lou - and to me, always in mental agony, in the perpetual search for peace within myself. Really, this is only my guess about who Tom really was. Who can fathom the intricacies of a human being? I also know that within him there were impulses of rebellion, actual bursts of it had flashed thunderously and mightily and then subsided quickly like summer storms. He had one of those bursts when he got his draft notice. He realized that it threatened his life and his hopes of domestic happiness with Mary Lou. He right away joined a group of draft-resisters and burned his draft-card together with theirs. Then the next day he reported to the induction center.

John Carson, Tom's father, once the colors of the tiny flag on his son's grave faded out and the flowers in the wreaths had decomposed in the fall rains, he sold his business and nobody saw him ever again. Tom's death just made my inclination for peace grow deeper. You see, dear dad, I can't help having in me the thought of "that being which in existing is infinitely concerned about his existence." Where did it come from? I don't know. At first it was a concern for my own life. When I found a few answers for my subjective concern, it evolved into the objective one and I began scrutinizing life itself. I wanted to find the truth of it, bitter or sweet that it turned out to be. Is life worth living? Its insurmountable limits, cradle and grave are atrocious and many of its aspects detestable. There is only the choice: take it as is or leave it. Nobody is forbidden to wonder: If life's duration is only an instant and also so painful, wouldn't nothing at all be better! As it is, the product of cosmic accidents, he is wise who takes it in the same vein and takes a chance with it, in a spirit of adventure. It didn't have a meaning at the outset, it cannot gain any now or ever. "May the promotion of what belongs in the field of our professional duties; not wife, children and family; not wealth, learning or power, nor higher standards of living for all men, not one of these things nor all of them together can ever make life meaningful." Once one has accepted it for what it is, without the illusion of a metamorphosis, one can live it as a wonderful adventure.

Chapter II

Right after Tom's death Mary Lou stopped going to church. I was going through a soul searching time myself, There was no doubt in my mind that if we were born in a-religious families we wouldn't have religious problems at all. I asked her if Tom's death had anything to do with it. She answered me that it had only a bit to do with it. Her objections were her own. Mary Lou went on explaining to me how people go to church not to open their hearts to God, but to get rid of their burdens and responsibilities. They go to church to thrust their personal, moral, political and economic responsibilities on the priest's shoulders so that they can live their lives as irresponsible children. But she also had contempt for the clergy. None of them had spoken against the war as far as she was concerned. She mentioned Cardinal Spellman with disgust. For a moment Mary Lou had become too loquacious. Tom's death really had precipitated a vast change in her life. Then she went back to put the blame on everybody: The Church for failing itse great responsibility to lead the flock, and the flock for being apathetic in the present flux of events. I told Mary Lou not to blame everyone, that the flock never leads. It wants to be led. We know that to make the right decisions, we must have a vast amount of knowledge, availability of data and infinite wisdom. As it's written: "In much wisdom is much grief : and he that increaseth knowledge increaseth sorrow." And if the majority avoid sorrow, should we really expect them to want it increased?

We ask , therefore, to be relieved of the burden of decision-making, by thrusting it upon the Church, the State, the Enterprise. How many times have we who have taken up our share of the burden, weary and confused, willingly accepted a friendly hand, its ease of our unbearable load! At the many impasses in uncharted regions of thought and action, we would all welcome as a blessing the pointing finger of the sage indicating toward the right direction. Unfortunately there has never been either a friendly hand or charitable help in word or sign. We have to take risks and assume responsibilities. You, Mary Lou, frail and fragile little girl, dear friend of mine, have chosen a difficult and thorny road! I wish you all the luck in the world for success, wishing to see you at the end of the long, long road!

In our culture, conscientious men rarely

survive with their ideals intact. Girls have to surmount more obstacles than men, and their chances to reach the goal without compromising their ideals or their bodies, are very slim. I accompanied Mary Lou home and comforted her as best as I could. I wished I had been empowered to do good whenever and wherever it was needed; to heal every bleeding heart, to take away the troubles of every let down man and woman! I realized that somebody had tried to do all that and for that reason was crucified many centuries ago as a malefactor. And yet, failures cannot stop us from trying to add our own little stone to the building of civilization.

Mary Lou's father, like any other father of a young girl, didn't like any boy who got close to his daughter. He tolerated Tom, but would have liked me to be her boyfriend now. He had noticed Mary Lou's change of attitude and her sorrow. He thought that I could snap her out of it, as her old friend. In his laconic way, he adored her, wishing to see her happy. I couldn't help him in that way. Really having grown up together Mary Lou and I were too much like brother and sister, and alike in temperament and otherwise, to be romantically attracted to each other. We found pleasure in being together, but our casual contact of flesh, didn't have any sparks of passion. We had gotten as close as any lovers but nothing had ever happened and that was the test. Passion and love have reticence and limits.

You can't express your love easily to the loved one; your emotion seals your lips. Evidently I was not in love with Mary Lou because I felt at ease, either talking or getting very close to her. My flesh wasn't stirred by the irresistible forces of love that warns a lover to stay a little far from the loved one because if he gets too close his emotions will get out of control and a crash is inevitable. I didn't know if I was ever going to meet a girl who would make me feel like that and set my heart on fire. I knew that she wasn't Mary Lou. I sensed that she felt likewise and looked beyond me. We were walking toward the future in separate ways. I could no longer stick around without undermining her future. I wished her good luck in finding the good man she deserved or in any case a fulfilling life.

After all these years, I still remember her family's white Cape Cod house amidst the magnolias as familiar to me as our lovely also white Cape under the most beautiful poplar, always on my mind. Is it still there, dad?

Nationalism, the powerful drive to dominate, the urge to have one's own nation, one's own state assert itself above, over, and at the cost of others.

—Huizinga

Chapter III

Since Biblical times we have records of economic cycles, of a 7 year period -7 years of plenty followed by 7 years of scarcity. During times of economic crest, rulers, throughout the ages have used their wealth to wage war. The riddle of it is still with us. Whereas in an agricultural economy the downward trend was spelled by scarcity a consequence of under-production, nowadays over-production and unemployment seems to cause it. At any rate, mutatis mutandis, the 7 years 1965-71 were of economic crest for our nation, affluent years. We used their surplus to wage war in South-East Asia. Then, as the casualties mounted, an unsuspected event happened. A few young people formed a core of a movement of protest to the war and refused to be drafted. Like an avalanche corning down the valley, it grew to such an immense proportion to become a serious obstacle to our war-mongers and dispensers of death.

This peace movement crossed the oceans and appeared in Europe, and here and there around the world. And the earth, astonished, saw its best children, against the trend of immemorial savagery, marching unarmed, holding hands, orderly, singing songs of love and peace in the first and perhaps the last apogee of the human race in vindication of life against the methodically planned annihilation of millions of human beings in order to promote ideologies, interests, hegemonies, pride, etc.

The old, with their callous butcher's minds stuck to their lethal guns, and in the end, crushed it with a sigh of relief of challenged monsters, which for an instant, saw imperiled their ferocious pursuit of human sacrifice. Now they can relax and plan for tomorrow the usual carnage. To escape the imminent a handful of us fled abroad. A few of us survived; where are the rest? They vanished as if swallowed up by the earth in a silent cataclysm. The abstract State that never sleeps has no feelings, no consciousness, has devoured them after having discredited them with the help of provocateurs, priests, secret agents, informants and other means used by despots and in totalitarian stakes.

We behaved like fools because we were victims of a democracy that never was and made of propaganda, fed to us with our first pabulum. Lying teachers, books full of lies; rhetoric of demagogues night and day who blasted into our heads

through the media of radio, T.V. newspapers,
magazines and what not, made fools of us. A <u>1984</u>
or worse political environment, like quicksand lay
under our feet, while we walked naively on it as if
it were solid rock. The murderers saw us for what
we were, what they had purposefully made us,
simpletons. With their loaded guns, truncheons
in hand, they saw us approaching in groups hand
in hand in plain day light, to assemble peaceably, according to the Constitution, and voice our
grievances, We were shot at, beaten, spat upon,
jailed, treated worse than criminals and labeled
enemies of our country.

It was a beautiful morning-Spring had come
at last. The bright sun was shining through the
pastel-green of the tender leaves of the sycamores
that ornamented a11 the streets of the suburbs,
through which I was driving in my old Chevy.
I reached park-scarce Cambridge, and luckily parked in a side street, half a mile away from
the Cambridge Common. The rally was to take
place there and then move to the Boston Com-
mon-How many were we there that morning?
We left the counting to those who kept us under surveillance: the police in uniform, the secret
agents in plain clothes, the informers posing as
photographers, provocateurs donning our casual
style attire and such like, pillars of law and order. We walked hand in hand, boys and girls, de-

rided, insulted, and at close range punched by the not so civil and not so silent majority. Their solid masses formed banks to our streaming throng, ready to form a dam to stop us from reaching the place where we were to assemble peaceably. They showed us their burning eyes and faces full of hatred, as if we were armed vandals ready to destroy civilization with our elemental fury.

They of course, thought of themselves as being on the side of civilization. Human blood, meanwhile was dripping down their not so civilized hands. We could have been the blossoms of spring, reorienting the culture of our country, and perhaps of the world, toward life and the rediscovery of human concerns. How naive we were to believe that we could alter the conscience of a nation inebriated by military glory! The stony disregard of our peaceful gatherings, of the mass clubbing and arrest, showed us that we were not just faced by a stubborn administration, but by a fake democracy. What we had loved and trusted, we found out to our dismay was nothing more than a whitewash of democracy covering up a repressive governmental system, where the democratic praxis was used, that was all. Too many of our people identify themselves, unconsciously perhaps, with this form of repression. Shall we conclude that our democracy will be lost if nobody rises to save it? Many more liberties will be lost in the future, but very few will notice their departure.

Anyway, we reached Boston Common, listened to four or five speakers expressing our moral indignation and our political grief. Then we sat on the grass. We emptied the pockets of our colorful threads of sandwiches and jelly-beans and soda cans, etc. Some of our group had carried along their infants and now began to feed them from nursing bottles. Most of us were students. There were some faculty-members, but not many. Whole squads of police- men had remained on the surrounding grounds, and officials in civil attire seemed to be in charge of the force. We were concerned that we'd be provoked and then force would be used against us. I sat next to a young brunette girl , all verve and at the same time full of poise. My first impression, relying on what she wore, and a certain uneasiness in her look was that she was there out of bravado. Then I realized that I had been unkindly judging her. Was it up to me to question by what destiny or virtue she had decided to join in a moral mutiny against an unacceptable war that bared a manipulated social and political reality? The fact that she was there, taking responsibility for the consequences that standing up for a just cause entailed. She then had my admiration. She'd bear the stigmata of rebellion for the rest of her life. How beautiful she

was in her lavender miniskirt that showed plenty
of her satin skin, much above her pretty knees.
Her white shirt followed her harmonious lines in
a voluptuous form bounded by her denim jacket.
All her body told me of meticulous cleanliness
and care. Her brown eyes told me of her gentle
disposition. I stared at her lovely face, her lovely
body, and I liked every inch of it. Certainly her expensive, pretty clothes contrasted with the rough
threads of the crowd, I had a foolish resentment
toward her showing so much of her lovely flesh, to
everyone. I wanted it all for myself. Til then, I had
only dreamed of the girl of my life. She had the
vagueness of the ideal. And now, she was here in
all the splendor of her flesh entrancing my senses
and my mind. Somehow, I knew, from the depth
of my being, that this was the girl of my destiny.
I could go naked for want of clothes with no roof
above my head, wandering for the rest of my life
as a perennial nomad; a clown pitching my tent
wherever a few pennies could be collected by
"*faire epanouir la rate du vulgaire*" I could stand
all that and more, but I couldn't live without her.
I tried to spare her some indignities that most of
us had gone through.

A week before, another rally had been broken
up by provocateurs. The police intervened and
we were clobbered. I was left on the grass with a
fracture on the right side of my head, just above

the ear. After these many years, dear dad, I still feel an excruciating pain on my head at the least change in the weather. I knew that that kind of storm was approaching, and wanted my beautiful girl to escape it by leaving early. I suggested, without alarming her, that it be a good idea, if she went back home as it was getting dark and her parents surely would worry about her; besides, there was no point for her staying as there was nothing more to be done for the day. I was as I found out later, one year older than she, having turned eighteen two months earlier. While I was attracted to her, was she attracted to me? I never was good-looking. I had resigned myself to my looks, but how I wished I were good-looking at that moment. Looks aren't everything, but they are visible. Our personality, our knowledge, whatever is in us, takes a long time, if ever, to be known to others. Now, there was my chance for happiness, and it hinged on my physical appearance. My chances were very slim, that she'd be attracted to me. What was I seeing of her? Was it her mind and her thoughts? No. I was seeing the shape of her legs, the brown of her eyes, the curves of her body. She also was seeing my exterior. I offered to walk her home. My secret wish was that we'd walk together, hand in hand, for the rest of our lives. You see, dear dad, I have never done things worth while in my life in a half way, but always all the way. I tacked the ocean from one continent to the other, come what may! I have never taken short tacks close to shore or only on sunny days, and the ocean blue and serene.

Walking with the most beautiful girl in the world, I talked and talked. I bared to her all my dreams and my concerns, all my hopes. If she believed that they defined the contours of my being she would accept or reject me, for what I really was. While I exposed myself entirely, I used restraint questioning her. I wanted to know everything about her, but only if she volunteered to let me know. If she knew finesse and I was sure she had a lot of it, she'd appreciate my discretion, I learned that she lived with her widowed mother and an older brother, Steve. Her father had died in 1952, in Korea. She was a year old then, therefore had no memories of her father at all." I went to the rally against the war because it kills a lot of people and creates destruction and misery; not particularly because my father was killed in war," she told me. Her voice that, so far had been calm and even, spiraled to an emotional crescendo.

She couldn't understand why her father, with a wife and two babies had volunteered for the war. She paused for a moment and lifted her lovely eyes to the last purple of the sky, and added, that her father went to war either because he was infinitely unhappy, or was bored to death, she said that in a muffled voice, as if talking to herself. I intuitively took her hand in mine in a comforting effort. She didn't retrieve it. We walked, I happily, hand in hand with her, for many blocks. We crossed the Charles River, and were back in Cambridge, walking on Mass, Ave. We reached the side street where in the morning, I had parked my old Chevy, I asked her if she lived far from there. She answered that she lived right at that street. I saw a lucky omen in having parked my jalopy a few feet from her home. Then I wondered if she would let me come in. She said that, of course I could come in. She lived in a massive building with a high brick-wall and a huge elaborate wrought-iron gate. We entered through that gate, crossed a long courtyard, with a splashing fountain in the middle. To my eyes of all things, this resembled the Alhambra I had seen in a geography book. Up the wide staircase, I saw many corridors, and I thought that I was in a small royal palace. I told her, that in my jeans, I wasn't in proper attire for being presented to her royal family. She laughed heartily at my mentioning that she was royalty. She said that she was a commoner and they occupied only an apartment suite in the building. The entire estate belonged to Howard Tomson, a distant relative. He was a banker, who had avoided the foreclosure of the building, had become their benefactor, and they were now his hostages. I detected by the tone of her voice that she hated Mr. Tomson. Before entering her home, I considered that if she was going to introduce me to her family, she had to know my name. I told her that meeting her had been the most beautiful event of my life. That I'd like to see her again and again. I announced I was Anthony Gerald. She answered that she'd like to see me again, and her name was Laura Cabot- Laura then preceded me as we entered a small study where a robust and fair haired young man, was sitting on a brown and messy sofa.

She introduced me to him as her brother Steve. While Laura was all verve, Steve had the attributes of a-historical people who don't bother with time and don't let it bother them. Corpulent if not overweight, with a powerful voice to match, he had a gentle disposition, I soon found out. He was interested in everything but devoted to nothing in particular. Specialization, he thought leads to work and he detested work. I later learned that he knew how to make theoretically, a home-made atom bomb with a kg. of Plutonium 210, a kg. of Uranium 238 and a charge of dynamite, but he wouldn't go to MIT. He had enough economic information to correct the most appalling flaws of our monopoly- ridden system, but wouldn't touch it with a ten foot pole. He was at home in architecture, literature, law and anything that is listed in any respectable library. Steve asked Laura if she'd been at the rally in a reproachful tone. When she answered, in a casual way that yes she had been there, Steve was much irritated with her. Then Laura asked me if I'd like a cup of coffee. I was delighted to have been asked. She took my jacket and put it away, with hers, in a closet by the door. Then she went in the kitchen to turn on the percolator. She came back and the two of us sat on that messy sofa next to Steve. I assumed that he liked me from the start and no sooner was speaking to me in a fatherly way perhaps he was patronizing me in the same way he was doing with his sister. He told me that we were silly fools, like all the others who went to the anti-war rallies marching right into the trap set by the police dopily and in broad daylight to be easily branded by the secret agents who recorded who we were, what we said and would then prosecute us. Steve called us innocent babies. He surprised me and rebuked us all for not having revolted in secret as the freemasons of old, the secret societies, the underground movements. He concluded that, from now on we had no future. I told him that we weren't true rebels plotting underground to over-turn our government, but rather to restore the integrity of our Constitution that had been violated. We all rallied in the open in front of our countrymen in plain daylight and we assembled peaceably as it was our right to do to voice our grievances toward an administration that, using a false pretext had led us in an undeclared war on Vietnam. The administration alleged, and was later disproved, that one U.S. Destroyer was attacked by the Vietnamese navy in the Gulf of Tonkin. Our young men in the armed forces were fighting and dying not for our country but for a lie. There was a clear case in my mind for impeaching President Lyndon B. Johnson, and reprimanding the Congress for being fooled so easily. But impeachment was never mentioned, and Congress was never censured, so we took to the streets to stop the unjust war.

My explanation, I thought, disposed Steve toward our cause. Because he knew almost everything about everything, I asked him, that given that in our national history we don't have a precedent of what kind of punishment would be meted out to an impeached president besides removal from office, and likewise for the members of Congress who transgressed the Constitution. Steve's answer was that there was no provision in the Constitution besides the removal from their office. I insisted to him that we needed to , therefore, fill those omissions and soon. " Then Congress ought to pass two laws or Constitutional amendments that specify the penalties for those violations. Will Congress do that and soon?" I remember asking naively. Steve doubted it. As things now stood, he admonished his sister and me to be alert from the attacks on us, now prey to vultures. I confided to Steve that I would stay put and suffer and fight for my rights and beliefs to the end of the earth if Laura came with me. Luckily for me, Laura didn't hear my blurted declaration of love for her, so soon, as we had just met, because she was still in the kitchen making the coffee. Steve listened with a smile of approval to my blurting out my love for his sister, and put his friendly arm around my shoulder. Next I had the best cup of coffee of my life, with the girl that I loved, and my new friend, Steve. From that day on, I couldn't stay away from Laura's door. Steve, the next time I was back to take Laura on a date told me that Tomson whom he disliked, was standing in my way to happiness. In his opinion Laura had deliberately compromised herself politically in order to free herself from old Howard Tomson. According to Steve, Laura thought that Howard, with his conservative principles, wouldn't ever marry a girl with radical views which really were unacceptable in his circle. Casually I asked Laura if she truly believed in our cause or if it was a means to escape Tomson's pursuit. She was hurt by my doubt about our cause, and told me that she held her ideals as dear as I did and even more so. I asked her to forgive me, and we reconciled and we kissed for the first time.

When I took Laura back home, Steve asked her if she knew Amanda Buckley. Laura didn't know the girl, and asked her brother how he had met the girl. Steve shrugged off the question and told her that Amanda was his last night date. He went on describing her. Middle height, well-built, delicate rosy skin, red long hair, and according to him, green eyes that appeared as always lost in reverie or aimed vaguely at nothing- and shallow. Then Steve told his sister that he was going to take Amanda out again the next night. Laura asked her brother why if he didn't care for Amanda, was he having another date with her? Steve said that he was doing that for two reasons - First, because it was his mother's idea, Amanda's father was a big-wheel at Harvard - Second, because Tomson had arranged those dates. His mother and Howard told him to look at his future, and encouraged him to throw a line where money could be caught. Steve's real reason was, I assumed, that he liked Amanda's body, but had no choice but to take the little mind that went with it.

Chapter IV

Dear Dad, you know, as well as I do, that thought arises when obstacles are in one's way or when one wants to see the other side of things notices inconsistencies, finds given answers although convoluted, beautiful unsatisfactory etc. Accumulation of information, without critical appraisal, is a mnemonic feat, which will result in an accumulation of pieces of different puzzles that obviously will never fit together or believing in a ready-made ad hoc scenario, with its backdrop in three fake dimensions as if they were real. Amanda, if Steve was right, was a firm believer in the clean-cut scenario of life, where the winds blow in the desired direction, the sky's always blue, the State always stands for the universal good; education can only be acquired at Ivy-League colleges; dissent is always evil, etc. It will never occur to her that it was devised and painted by someone who also used it to bend people to be actors in his play, puppets in his hand; that many things that are said on stage, some reflect reality, but many more don't; that life's many times more complex than any play; that heroes are made of the substance that the author is made of. Often that substance is poisonous to life, while that of the villain's is on the side of life, and for this reason he is persecuted, tormented, executed. The villain's demise is welcomed and applauded by Amanda and other spectators like her. Then Steve told us that Amanda was crazy about horror movies. Was it coincidental?

However, what Amanda Buckley believed and liked, was irrelevant to me. It was what Laura Cabot believed in, that I was interested. Now that Steve had brought up the subject, I saw my chance to probe into his sister's aspirations and ideals. I didn't expect a full revelation of her character, but a good portion of it I already knew, only a bit more of it. Nobody can fathom the depth of another human being. I probed for a tiny sample and asked Laura, what did she expect from life. To you, dear dad, that question to my dear young lady, might sound impertinent. Now as I had already said what I expected from life during our long first walk together, my question was fair. Laura took her time before giving me an answer. She said that she expected to get her fair share of it. If life had no ultimate purpose transcending it, she'd live completely and usefully, earning her daily bread, contributing in the effort toward perfecting society and helping her fellow man.

She expected to pay her dues while claiming her rights. She planned to live according to her tastes, but short of self-indulgence, to be attractive and stimulating to a good young man, and being attracted and stimulated by him.

She wanted to get married at the proper time. She had to love her future husband and he her immensely because it had to endure for life, walking together, hand in hand to the end. It wouldn't be boring, rather interesting, and always desirable and as the years went by, life apart from one another would be unbearable, even for a brief while. Laura concluded that those were a few of the things she expected from life and would consciously strive for. She added that unconsciously she had more wishes, more desires, more dreams, more vistas, more ephemeral things; things of beauty, valley dawns and sunsets always different but always wonderful. Laura added that she loved and appreciated all the arts and had a complex love-hatred with the ocean, She couldn't stay away from it, even for a while, missing gliding on its expanse. She surmised, this love-hate perhaps came down to her from a long line of ancestors, who spent most of their lives on its waves as whalers. A few of them were swallowed by it, when it became wild and destructive. Dad, how do you like Laura so far? There is more of her.

She also told me that she had urges that tor-

mented her body; others that pushed her into
crowds and others that set her apart. She wondered from where they came together to her or
how she at the same time also acquired this longing for good laws, fair distribution of the goods
of the earth, her compunction for ethics. Laura
thought that most of her character was molded
by her family's tradition she was born into which
had a double strand of whalers and judges as the
Cabots had been both. She loved to listen to cho-
ruses and full orchestras, and delight in baroque
quartets. She liked sincere people, good books,
any form of art that supplied her with pleasure
and thought. Laura thought that appreciation of
good people and good things is learned, but to
discover how good they are, is this ability innate?
She liked to create, to make things, but also to
waste time doing nothing, just dreaming,.Good,
I thought, that Laura's character' s , not so impul-
sive as mine. She would apply the brakes on me,
thus complimenting our future decision- making
on the slopes of our life together. And I would
have liked to tell her that, but I couldn't. She reiterated that married to the man that she loved, it
would be painful for her to stay apart from him
for interminable hours, either because of holding
jobs in different places or just staying home, waiting for him. She would rather work together with
him and be close night and day. She complained

that our economic system, doesn't give a chance, to a man and a woman in love to work together in the same endeavor, under the same roof, side by side. Steve did not agree with his sister's wish, "too much togetherness, " he laughed heartily, agitating the springs of the sofa we three were sitting on to the rhythm of his laughter. He told his sister that what to her seemed a fault to him was a redeeming factor. In his opinion, not seeing one another for eight or nine hours helped any couple to stay together, giving them a respite. Laura huffily replied that he was entitled to his opinion, but she'd stick to hers. Then Laura blurted out to my delight, that she wished I were the man she'd liked to be with, night and day, every night and every day. Steve wasn't surprised at his sister's pronouncement of her love for me. He knew that we were in love. He smiled at us with consent but said nothing, knowing that our dream wouldn't come true, as long as Tomson was there in the picture. He had been in the picture before me, and yet, I thought that time was on my side and against him. I could see Tomson courting the widow rather than her daughter. It's also true that I would have hated any other man, young or old, who could have put my dreams of love in jeopardy by putting himself between Laura and me. At any rate, who was Howard T. Tomson? If I believed Steve and his critical appraisals, the Tomsons were Nantucket whalers, When the whaling industry was displaced by the oil wells, the Tomsons left the island in search of their fortunes on land. His grandfather didn't have much success. His father, as a sixth grade teacher, was able to scratch enough money together before dying, to send his son to Amherst and Harvard. From there he made it on his own. This, according to Steve, was the public version. The real facts were that Howard T. Tomson was a clever rascal who early in life, cut part of his soul out to fit it to the requirements of the system, and the juxtaposition had come out perfectly. Many could swear that he came into big money when he was still an adolescent, by deliberately introducing his widowed mother, a still young and very attractive Irish blonde, for whose love his father had converted to Catholicism, to an old coal tycoon by the name of M.T.Steinberger. He and his mother worked so well on the old man, that at his death he left the bulk of his fortune to Howard and his mother, and only pennies to his two sons. While we were chatting, Laura's mother came home, accompanied by Howard T. Tomson.. Agatha Venestir Cabot, enveloped by an aura of makeup and perfume, I guessed, was forty. She was the older, spitting image of Laura, more sophisticated and experienced, of course, in dealing with the world she was born into and had lived all her life. It was a small, precious world, glamorous, superficially attractive, but of little reality. Tomson was exactly as Steve had described him: in his middle forties, about six foot, blond receding hair, blue eyes, simply attired as an undertaker.

Then, we all adjourned to the living room, and I was formally introduced to Agatha and Howard. They perceived by my manner and jacket and blue jeans that I did not belong to their world. I suspected that Tomson wouldn't have liked me even if I were a member of his world. In a short time he brought up how much he disliked the shabby appearance of young people; especially young girls in coarse jackets and worn out blue jeans. He thanked God that Laura was still wearing her finery, and disgustingly couldn't stop staring at her legs that her yellow miniskirt, while seated, had only receded further still revealed up to her lovely thighs. Modestly she tried to minimize the exposure by crossing her legs, but there was still much left in the open, 1 reluctantly guessed that there was no harm done by watching although I knew that the old philanderer wanted much more than watching. If Steve was right, Laura wasn't the first teenager that Tomson was infatuated with, nor would she be the last. It seems there was a pattern, He loved them from sixteen to nineteen. The moment they reached their twentieth birthday, he lost interest in them. Only this time,

with his infatuation with Laura, marriage was
mentioned. I wasn't going to analyze the mental
problems of that man. I only wanted to deliver
Laura from his grip. When the demonstrations
against the war were mentioned, Tomson de-
clared he was one hundred per cent for the war
and it would be right, to put into concentration
camps all the "beatniks" that opposed it. He made
a convoluted speech interspersed with ex-cathe-
dra pronouncements, on our role as defenders of
freedom for the entire world, of the need to bomb
to smithereens any nation that opposed our humanitarian purpose. His enthusiasm for the idea
of killing, his hatred toward those who opposed
the war and for real humanitarian concern, his
carnal indulgence, his quick foreclosures of those
in distress who fell behind their mortgage payments were inconsistent with his professed piety,
notwithstanding his punctual church-service at-
tendance, his biblical quotations, and his well as
his advertised large contributions.

Was Tomson's portrayal that I made for you
unfair, dear dad? I tried to be as impartial as I
could, but couldn't find a noble side of him. There
was and is in front of me an unscrupulous, immoral
man that I rightly detested. How many Tomsons
were and are still there polluting civilization? I
guess more than a few. We can place them in two
separate, but not by much, groups. One com-

posed of those who have made a lot of money, or inherited a lot of it, and made some more; have been exposed to a splash of culture, use a fastidious language, to cover up their shallow knowledge and the perennial holier than thou in their hearts; who think of themselves as more civilized than the rest. Made arrogant by their success, always material, they are antinomians, who forget that, whatever they've accomplished was made possible by the use of the commonwealth's infrastructure and not by themselves in the primeval jungle, but in a physical and human environment created by many generations' sacrifices of which they fail to take notice and give credit. The other group includes those who concur in the shallow thinking and in the prejudices of the first group, but haven't a great deal of money to their names; as a matter of fact have to eke out a living by hard work. These are minuscule property-owners but colossal conservatives. They were persuaded by the rich masters for whom they slave, that masters and employees work together for the benefit of all, thus with their labor they are upholding the ideals of their progenitors: the Pilgrims.

Tomson tested me on my station and status. He found both negligible, because I didn't feel superior to other people, nor did I fear them. He was disgusted with me when I told him that I didn't worship money. His reply was that if I didn't have high ambitions I'd never amount to anything. He rose from his chair and came close to me and pointed his finger at me, and cried, how in the land of opportunity I was refusing to take advantage of it. He then reiterated ,"in my vernacular", as he put it, that I had no guts. In other words, Tomson had disqualified me to aspire to conquering the golden fleece, that is, Laura. I wasn't too ambitious to earn what was necessary to keep Laura in her accustomed style of life. What he didn't know was that I didn't crave for riches. I wanted rather to live a good life with Laura, in whatever economic means we could attain, be they modest or high, but we'd aimed highest at aesthetic and cultural splendor. Tomson wasn't quite yet through finding faults with me. Haven't I sometime seen you entering Christ Church, or more often Park Street Church and by chance Tremont Temple? He inquired, Then added: I don't know what to make of it. Are you Unitarian, Fundamentalist or Baptist? My answer was, that I was searching for the truth. That after Sputnik, Armstrong and company getting to the moon, the space exploration that let us expand the knowledge and vastness of the Universe, the electronic age, with its discoveries that are changing how we live; I began to analyze the axioms upon which our civilization was built and whether they were still valid. He was searching for what was still standing and what had to go. When the savior of Wellesley, that's where he lived, had spoken, I switched my attention to the lady of the house.

Chapter V

Agatha Venestir Cabot was neither better nor worse than any other woman born in a rich family, whose cares in life, were to know what to wear at different times and occasions; how to avoid ennui in gala performances, receptions, sports competitions; how to marry within her status circle. At Smith she had glossed over those very things so congenial to her own disposition for fun and games. She had also learned to appreciate the harmony of colors and sounds; the finesse of tones, the grace of contours and the mysterious beauty of refined things. Intellectual reflection, on the other hand, had escaped her. She couldn't conceive why some persons waste their lives, racking their brains to understand life, when one can easily enjoy it without giving a thought. Her appreciation of beauty cost her dearly when she fell in love and married a very good-looking, from an honorable family but penniless, young man. She had learned her lesson. Now, she wanted to be sure, sure that her daughter, didn't make her costly mistake. That her daughter's values differed from hers and money didn't have the preeminence she attached to it, didn't seem to matter to the widow. She believed that whatever gave her happiness would also give happiness to Laura. She wanted to marry her daughter to Tomson who'd provide her with the comforts of life. That Tomson's age, his life style, his philandering and personal idiosyncrasies could make her daughter miserable didn't enter her mind. She believed that money can heal all scars in the human heart and in the human mind. She was ready to sell her daughter at a good price, to vicariously fulfill her ambition. Anyone with a bit of common sense could see that Tomson's proposal of marriage was simply a move to break down Laura's resistence to his advances to sleep with her. Then after a while he would leave her in the same way he had done with all the other young girls. Agatha didn't see that or didn't want to see. Physically she was still beautiful, though she had a malicious look in her hazel eyes. She was a larger copy of Laura, that time had touched however slightly. Her curves were pronounced, but her delicate skin dazzled still with fleshy sensuousness in her well fitted grey gown. She moved and talked with a touch of refined elegance. I wondered how a smart woman like her, had accommodated to the awkward situation she was in. I had heard of mothers passing their lovers to their daughters, but this sort

of thing usually happened to those in the gutter
or in the highest places of society. In other words
among those who are either beneath or above mo-
rality. At least, the sophisticated think of themselves above it. Very stringent circumstances had
bent a proud woman like her to stoop that low. I
knew that Tomson had a good grip on her, due to
her financial distress. Lack of money can break
anyone's moral fiber. The appearance of this rich
and attractive relative of her late husband's at the
moment of need, rekindled the hope of realizing
her ambitions. A few years back she must have
been really beautiful, I thought. In my opinion,
dear dad, status had been the driving force in her
life. Love and decency don't last long when status
is lost. She might have regretted having married
Alfred S. Cabot, a decent man who got lost in
the vertigo of a restless industrial society. According to his daughter, he had the soul of an artist but before Korea had gotten buried away in
an office of a vast insurance company tabulating
digits so dry of any emotional content that, he
was afraid they'd dry up his very soul. Although
Agatha loved him, or had loved him in the past,
when passion had silenced her reason as the years
went by, she came to loathe the quiet man who
had given up his dreams and also the struggle to
be somebody in society. She had contempt for the
man of no importance she was married to. The

man that Agatha would have liked to be married to was this unscrupulous, rich relative. He'd have brought her back into her milieu of luxury and splendor of premieres, balls, elegance, savoir vivre, never having to worry about tomorrow again. I inferred that, things being as they were, Tomson did not go beyond making her his mistress and paying her bills. As time went by, she realized that she wouldn't catch her sly fish. She tried to catch any other of his caliber, but in vain, all the successful men she tried her luck with, were ready to go to bed with her, but with no strings attached. She stuck with Tomson, though she knew that he was unwilling to take her back to the promised land. Time went by unseen but felt. As a wife she only had had to manage staying healthy. Competition was held at a minimum, by the bond of matrimony and youth. As a mistress, she knew that she had to watch her figure carefully as her youth was in decline, competition was always present in her precarious relationship, open to one and all. Pretty soon she got into the habit of looking at herself, stark naked in the mirror, after taking a bath or shower. She was pleased to see that her body was still in full splendor. She adhered more strictly to her already strict diet. She feared competition and right she was. She had known of other women in his life.

Recently, however, her competitors were teenage girls. Tomson now preferred them very young. A while back he had kept Jean T. As soon as she reached her twentieth birthday, he replaced her with Joanna, her three years younger sister, Time meanwhile went by. One morning Agatha after taking her bath, looked at her body in the mirror and noted , here and there signs of the dreaded autumn of life. How time had flown away! Her children had also grown up. The hope that her ambitions would be realized were very slim. If only her six-teen year old daughter could realize them! Tomson who had seen Laura, from a child developed into a beautiful young lady, prodded her mother's ambitions for his own scheme; expecting to make her his next plaything. He promised that he'd introduce Laura into what her mother called, the beautiful world, by marrying her. You can see, dear dad, that I was an intruder in their scheme. But I could see clearly, that Tomson had no intention of marrying Laura; only of gratifying himself for a while, as he had done with the other teenage girls. People like him never marry. Besides, I knew that Laura wasn't going to be his mistress. I was eighteen, young with no social standing, no money, and an uncertain future. With such credentials I was a negligible rival to Tomson but could have become a formidable one if Laura meant it when earlier that evening, she stated that she was in love with me, I offered her true love, a clean life, and shared dreams that realized or not would sustain us throughout our unknown destiny.

Meanwhile, the haughty lady, never stopped talking about who was who, of immense fortunes incredible estates, yachts, horse-racing stables, private jets and such like. By the time I esteemed was time for me to leave, I hated her. Then, as she helped me with my jacket, I accidentally touched her upper arm. What an unsuspected pleasure I felt. It stirred in all my flesh a lust for her, that scared me. I also had a feeling that she had deliberately squeezed, however gently, my arm. In the emotional turmoil that I was in, I was not sure why had she offered to help me with my jacket when Laura could have done it. Was it to compromise me in front of her daughter? Then I dismissed it as a figment of my imagination. I kept going back to her house because I was in love with Laura, and yet, I had this thorn in my flesh that kept me sliding toward that hated woman. As I became more in love with Laura, I called on her whenever I had free time on my hands. Steve liked having me around. She, it seemed to me, didn't mind having me around, on the contrary, she had an ominous sparkle in her eyes whenever nobody else was around but me and she entered the living room, looking for who knows for what, in a revealing negligee, or in panties and bra, or with only one of these on and found me staring at her. She gasped in surprise and her rage flew high. I was an intruder in her own home that was true, but I couldn't help coming back there. They were my new family, as I was lonesome in our house, now that my mother was dead and you, dad , were away. Therefore, on my frequent visits at the Cabot's home made it possible, by accident, to see the lady of the house, almost naked, with her satin skin and her gracious curves a la Reubens and of the other old masters who liked to paint women at the peak of their splendor, just before the decline or autumn of their life sets in. She was still beautiful, and my heart pumped so fast that I was afraid it would explode. It was an awkward situation for both of us. I hated her but at the same time felt the urge to embrace her in order to sprinkle a little dew on my parched desire, provoked by the lustful revelation of her body. I grew up a little each time such incidents occurred as I learned how to cope with it, and keep my desire in check. The senior prom was getting near. I'd have liked to take Laura to it, but it was considered passee to attend one and only those we considered square went. Then, perhaps because Steve had a date with Amanda, Agatha Cabot unbelievably but true, asked me to escort Laura to the Opera the next Friday night, and afterward have dinner at Tomson's mansion in Wellesley.

It was a condescending gesture by Howard who, usually flew to Europe or New York, to attend an opera performance of Turandot at the Metropolitan Opera House rather that at the Boston Opera House. How beautiful Laura looked in a light blue gown! She was the most beautiful girl in the theater. Her mother in a black shimmering gown, so revealing a decollete, was the most elegant lady there. She made every man's head turn to have a look at her at intermission in the foyer, I enjoyed the pageantry and the stirring, oriental flavored music; the only grand opera of Puccini. With that beautiful music still fingering in our ears, we drove to Wellesley. Tomson's mansion was a perfect Federal building disfigured by an ugly portal of Ionic columns. The sloping front lawn gave it a sense of majesty. You could tell that it spoke of money rather than taste. We had supper in the vast dining room, hung with brocades and furnished with antique, Louis XVI furniture. The gilded mirrors, the glass-door cabinets, the silverware, and the monogrammed china, were shimmering under the beautiful Murano chandelier. A waiter served consomme d'asperges.. Then came venison a l'anglaise and trout aux truffle, Russian salad, while a maid filled the glasses with chambertin. For dessert we had pineapple charlotte meringue and Rhine wine. Then we were served Turkish coffee. Dear dad, is there a connection between our palate and our taste? In my personal case there could be one.

I eat the most simple things at the same time I am fond of the most exquisite sauces and perfect seasoning. In art I love the sober palette and the daring conclusions. I had an almost perfect night, almost, because of the grudging mood of Tomson toward me, besides his insipid remarks about which dishes stimulate sex the most, it was quite an experience to watch Tomson and the widow, eating glutinously, lingering on every bite, and at every sip, as if eating and drinking were the quintessence of life. They didn't eat for living, rather lived for eating- At the Opera performance, I noted in them the same attitude.

They didn't enjoy it as entertainment mixed with revelation of choices we make in life that the composer offers us with beautiful music. For them it was simply entertainment, without purpose or moral intent. Entertainment had become an integral part of their life perhaps life itself. Did I catch them at their ebb? Then my portrayal of them was unfair. People, like things, look differently in different circumstances. We should see them under blue skies, doing what they like best, rather than on stormy or menacing days, under pressure, toiling at hated tasks. However, I didn't have any hints that Tomson at times was a saint nor that the widow had convictions expatiating beyond luxury and entertainment. Certainly, at times we hold opinions and do things that, for a moment raise us to the pinnacle of heroism or sainthood, but we soon fall back into our usual comfortable opinions, and the same way of life that make our character. Our two characters in their usual style of life, and in their environment, were genuine rubbish. However, I remember with delight, the ride to Wellesley in the back seat of the Mercedes, with Laura at my side, holding hands and furtively kissing. Now and then, she hummed a tune from the opera. It was fun. At supper Laura ate without fuss, just to appease her hunger, I was pleased to see that she wasn't like her mother also in eating.

You, dear dad, can see as I did, that the divide between Tomson and the widow, and Laura and me, was wide and deep. Our aims, hopes, concern with the problems of our age also separated us from them. Then Tomson tried jumping over that invisible barrier. The four of us had passed into the vast living room. The widow went to sit at the piano and began to play rag time tunes. Tomson had already had a few glasses of champagne by then and began reminiscing about his youth with tales that bored us, but made him sob, all the while having more champagne. Then, he came near Laura, and dragging her by the elbow toward his bedroom cried-why didn't she like him. Fortunately he passed out between the door and the bed. The widow dismissed the incident as unusual, a result from Tomson's over-hospitable zeal, that made him drink more than usual. I knew for a fact, through Steve that Tomson was prone to succumb to champagne's intoxication more often than the widow had admitted. By the many portraits and picture of our host's mother, hanging in every room of the mansion arose a suspicion to the source of his problem of remaining single for life. We returned to Cambridge by cab. However, the attempt by Tomson to drag Laura into his bedroom, lowered more the esteem, already low that she had of him. His loss was my gain. It improved my chances of happiness with the girl I loved. .

Oh it is excellent to have a giant strength,
but it. is tyrannous to use it like a giant.

—Shakespeare

Chapter VI

Democracy, freedom, equality before the law, and in the pursuit of happiness are simply words that the wind dissipates if the government goes in a different way than that of the people , who elected it intended. Any administration, that for personal ambition or ideology fools the nation to go to unnecessary war, or restricts the citizens' Constitutional rights in my opinion, commits treason by failing to defend and uphold the Constitution. Its elected officials swore this before taking office. This deterioration in the purpose of our government shouldn't have happened. We had been warned by President Eisenhower. He knew what he was talking about, having been the commander of the armed force that conquered Europe, in World War II, that the alliance of government and the industrial-military complex, would subvert the aims of the national foundation. The state then becomes an abstraction, without human feelings and interests. The results are that life doesn't have standing of its own and its priority over everything else are gone, when the state is an abstract being, bent to a forever expansion of its empire by force, claims that supporting it in its perpetual endeavor for power and glory gives life scope and meaning. With this line of reasoning, if you happen to be a citizen of Switzerland, or Luxembourg, or any other small nation, that isn't and can't aspire to be an empire, you have nothing to live for.

This newly derived individual self-effacement in favor of the state, done not even in the moral vein of doing what is right but as a systematic attempt in distracting the minds of simple people from their real interests. The rulers found a way to easily rule. It has happened before. Nothing's new under the sun. This gospel was preached by apostles like Tomson. It is obvious that it didn't have anything to do with democracy. It had been tried in any other form of government wherever the cultural values had been so watered down, that judging between truth and falsehood, was beyond even those considered well educated. In the universal ignorance, the symbols, bare of reality and of its complexity, necessary to comprehend reality, were taken as dynamic reality itself. Policies, of course, are scaled down and grounded on maps. I don't belittle maps, they are useful when one knows what they stand for. The new apostles' color, let's say green, the territory of the nation. Then, those among them who have the ambition

of statesmen all they have to do is, according to
the new-gospel, extend that green on the map as
far as they can even on other continents. Simple,
isn't it? The poor in spirit will also succeed, according to this gospel. When the great political
brains have agreed on where to extend the green,
their task is to hand over the map with the new
additions, to the military. The latter, with the help
of the intelligence agencies, figure out the men
and hardware necessary for overcoming the resistance that the people of that territory would put
up. The propaganda machine is also set in motion,
painting the aggression as a crusade against the
aggressive action of the enemy trying to destroy
our beloved country, its glorious institutions, and
its peace-loving people. Therefore, as one must
now shirk sacrificing his life in the hour of national peril; no one is allowed to dissent; no one
is allowed discuss anything, in order not to give
away any secrets to the enemy. Therefore, information of any kind, already curtailed, is now labeled secret, and no one knows what's going on, in
the great tradition of the democratic institutions.
If the territory in question, where the destiny of
the country is to be decided, can be easily occupied, because its defenders are few or ill armed,
the military make a present of it to the politicians,
proudly saying: look what your money and our
blood, have bought you! Elaborate ceremonies

where the pride of conquest is tempered by phony displays of humility, and statements that nobody wanted to do it, but it had to be done for the good of all concerned, and in the cause of freedom, of course.

On the other hand, if fierce resistance is encountered, you take what you can. Simply mark a line in the yellow territory between what you have succeeded occupying and the part where resistance was fiercest North Yellow and South Green. If objections have been raised at home and abroad, the new apostles tell the people at home, the truth according to their gospel-it was done because of our national interests; also because our sacred mission is that of extending freedom to all mankind. We may perish in this effort or go broke, but nothing will deter us from our path of honor. They tell the world, defiantly and bluntly sticking to their formidable weapons: what do you want to do about it! In order to add weight to their arms and menacing words they ask the country for more money to be spent on more powerful weapons in defense of our freedom to do as we wish at home and abroad.

Tomson was so fatigued explaining these truths to us, that afterwards, he entered the house at 45 Williams Street right away to relax in the arms of the young mistress of the month, Dear dad, I bet that the mentioning of this incident, didn't cause any emotions in you. You had a string of them yourself, in the past. In our abstract thinking I abridged to the bone in our daily turgid flux of events, a mistress is a minute fact of life in a community. One or ten or fifty faceless mistresses, leave you cold, as the digits that enumerate them. There are no facts that make them come alive in flesh and blood, as suffering human beings. A mistress, in the eye of anyone is a flesh-pot, and it's assumed, she likes being what she is and doing what she does. When she kills herself, by driving off a cliff, because Tomson let her go, pregnant, we might even think that she did the right thing. Now I'll let you in on a secret to see whether the knowledge of it will leave you cold as the other eases. Tomson's mistress of that time I mentioned who he kept at Williams St.,was Mary Lou, the adolescent daughter of your good friend , my best friend from back in Arlington. You heard it right, I wonder where Mary Lou is now, with the great future Tomson opened up for her. Her father, Mr. Anderson, as I used to call him, must have found a lot of comfort in his old age knowing that she has fulfilled his dreams about her, as well as her own. I hope that she didn't jump off a cliff, like the preceding Tomson's mistress. This prostitution business is another moral disgrace in our great nation. Say hello to Mr. Anderson for me, dear dad, if he's still around. I still treasure

his good advise he gave me in his better times.
Apparently nobody gave his daughter any. In our
long conversation by the pond, Mary Lou, as I
recall, expressed more than once the wish, that
we two as we grew older and got more experience
in politics would run for the Senate. We dreamed
that when we turned into middle- age our task
would be helping the younger generation to find
their place in our country and make it better
yet. Mary Lou, my dearest friend, believed that
people were as good as she, her father, Tom, my
mother, and me. She soon found out that there
were few good persons around her. Tomson, who
could have been her protector, rather than helping the poor young girl in finding a place in society debauched her, and destroyed her future. The
moral and social responsibilities together with the
political, and many others, which make a human
being civiilized, were alien to Tomson. Indeed,
what's civilization, if not a process of making human beings more humane! Only in this sense,
culture and knowledge have a purpose and direction. Otherwise,why bother? If the vicious human being is to remain a beast, let him stay such.
We expect to see such a savage monster covered
in animal skins unkempt and brandishing a club.
More often you find them in suits, groomed , giving the impression of being civilized. Only on the
surface. How civilized are the scientists who toil

in making more homicidal weapons and means
of mass destruction? Should we forgive them as
they do not know what they do? They know very
well that they have created- Hell on earth, and
keep adding to it. You dear dad, say let's forgive
them! Forgiveness is accorded those who repent;
but the scientists, with a scanty exception, keep
on working on evil inventions and can't be for-
given. Somebody suggested that the Hippocratic
oath, should be extended to physicists at gradu-
ation. But if education hasn't taught them that a
simple oath, won't deter them from their criminal
disposition. The solution would be to pack them
up, and throw the away the key.

Going back to Mary Lou, her fall was a puzzle
to me. How could it have happened? Were drugs
involved in her downfall? Many of the young people I knew had succumbed to drugs freely distrib-
uted by we didn't know who, perhaps in the effort
to eliminate the dissenters by any means. Was
Tomson involved in narcotics? I'd never know. I
refuse to believe that Mary Lou took to drugs, in
order to stick to her dreams rather than facing reality. I more realistically think that she was victim
of foul play. Anyway, by the fact that a few dissenters took to drugs the establishment tried to
discredit the whole peace movement as a pack of
drug-addicted, escaping into a never-never land
unprepared to cope with reality. The emphasis on

reality was so worked out by the establishment, as if it is a single category. In that way those who didn't submit to its dictates, would appear to be lunatics, rather than dissenters to the will of the rulers. They stigmatized them as abnormal; that they went against nature and the cosmic order of things. Thus, the unchangeable reality of nature was deliberately extended to that of human origin. By this gimmick, the human made environment, assumed the status immobile of the natural, physical environment. The fact that the artificial human environment, was created by human effort wasn't mentioned and consequently, the notion that it can be, has been instantly altered, by the same human effort, was artfully disregarded as infinite silliness or a demented effort to change the unchangeable, the eternal sameness. They branded it: the quintessence of idealistic stupidity. Thus ruminating on my way home, I was more determined than ever, to avoid that Mary Lou's fate would be extended to Laura.. My life depended on it. To Tomson, for reasons embedded in his troubled psyche, my presence in the picture stimulated even more his stubbornness, to have her. The challenge that I posed to him made the pursuit sweeter.

The next day, Tomson invited me for a ride in his Mercedes. As he usually gave this kind of ride to the young girls he was pursuing, I declined the invitation. Jokingly, I told him that he was not my type. He, who never smiles, pursed his lips in a nuance of a grin, and answered:"Touche!" It was a magnificent car and not the one in he had taken us to Wellesley the night of the Opera or the two other occasions I had been invited to his home. It was silver, with red upholstery. It was too feminine for my taste. On the other hand it was intentionally feminine, for its purpose was to allure and ensnare adolescent girls in it. Tomson asked me again to hop in for a ride as he wanted to discuss a few important things with me. I got in the car, reluctantly. We headed for the country. The tone of his voice was studied, persuasive, and I suppose the same he used on girls. On me it was irritating, as I smelled its phony quality, a mile away. He began talking vaguely of time, respon-sibilities, mortgage-payments and other fetters, that shackle prematurely, before young people can see the heavy burden those cares have put on their lives, before having had a little fun, and before their youth is gone. Then he told me that he, as an adolescent, had had, like all adolescents his own wild dreams. Then the years brought him to his senses. He realized that life must be lived rather than dreamed away- Everyone has to see more than one place, have more than one girl, try more than one job: before settling down. Puppy love as anybody knows, lasts no longer than a sea-

son. Then, he continued, his wisdom grew, and he
left the up on the clowns Fairyland, and landed
on factual ground. He exhorted me that I was too
young to settle down, That I should forget Laura,
and play the field; should see the world, before
binding myself to any woman, and spend my entire life in a dull corner of the world like this. He
offered me money, considered a loan for a gift or
as a token of his affection: whatever suited my
personal sensitivity. I, who have never hurt anyone felt the urge to punch him in the mouth, to
stop him in his attempt to bribe me with money,
under the euphemism of it being a loan to me.
After a brief pause he resumed his effort. He told
me what I already knew, that is, that Laura had
no money and he paid her family's bills. He reminded me that her ancestry had money! prestige,
and a historic background. Unfortunately, Alfred
Cabot, Laura's father in his genes didn't inherit
the knack of acquiring money himself. As a matter of fact he squandered whatever he had inherited. He wasn't in Tomson's opinion of that class
of people, but an artist at heart. He added, with
contempt, that those people hardly make money.
Then he switched to Steve. He had to agree that
Steve was a bright young man, that had in him
what it takes do become a big wheel in industry,
politics, science, you name it, but he would not go
to MIT or Harvard. He kept on reading all kinds

of books, and watching T.V, seated on that rotten sofa and never gave a thought to going out and making some money. He had to mention the loan for the family bills, course, that he paid. Being a relative, though a distant one, he had to. Lowering his voice, he confided in me that he himself had been poor, and therefore sympathized with his relations in distress. Poor Tomson, regretted, that he had to put his shoulder to the grindstone to make some money ,and to get where he was now. He swore to me that he would never be poor again. In a quivering voice he told me:"You have been taught that money's the root of all evil. Don't believe it. It's poverty that's the root of evil. You, however, don't necessarily have to put your shoulder to the grindstone, not right now. " I saw it coming that he would offer me money, and he could go to hell, as far as I was concerned. To have me out of his way and continue his pursuit of Laura as his mistress, now he pretended to be my mentor. As such he offered me money and advice. The few thousands that he'd give me to get out of his way he said, were a loan that I could pay back, when I became rich and famous. His advice was to go to Europe. To spend time in London, Paris, Berlin, and I shouldn't miss to go to Naples. I could have a lot of fun there. It would be for me a learning trip. I'd see the wonders that I found there and know how to build wonders of my own,

I'd come back with a wide intellectual and practical Knowledge on how to make a fortune, how to set up a bank, a factory, develop new inventions, employ hundreds or thousands of people. If going overseas didn't appeal to me, why wouldn't I go to the South or West of our country. For a young man like me, Las Vegas was the right place. I could become a Casino owner and have money and all the beautiful women I wanted. Then he added, that somebody, poor Mary Lou, I guess had told him, that you, dear dad, had fought in Korea, loved adventure, and wars and he suggested that I follow in your footsteps, join the armed forces, and become another Eisenhower or Patton. Tomson wanted me out of his way at any cost.. The hint wasn't enough, he was specific in his intent that I, away in Paris or Las Vegas, or in the armed forces, would forget my puppy love for Laura. It tells you that he didn't know me at all. I never give up what I want or believe in, as long I want it or believe in it.

In the meantime , driving on Route 2, we reached Concord. At the Walden Pond exit, Tomson took it. He parked the car and we descended to the pond. We walked on the path leading to where Henry David Thoreau's cabin , once stood. While walking, Tomson never stopped disparaging Walden's author. He advised me not to follow in Thoreau's steps. According to him, Thoreau had wasted his life pursuing impossible dreams. When we got to the site, we only saw a slab of granite, where the hearth once stood, as the only remainder of the cabin. Tomson cried aloud, that Thoreau could not build a cabin, grow beans, or live there alone. He spent most of the time in Concord, bothering Emerson, his own parents, and their neighbors. Dad, by what I've been telling you about Tomson, you get the idea, that he, like you, didn't like idealists, artists, or authors. I thought, he didn't read much either. Anyway, climbing out of Walden Pond, he resumed inveighing against Thoreau, that among other things he wouldn't pay taxes, was uncivil because we all know, that taxes are contributions to sustain the institutions and the infrastructure that let us live in the community and in peace. Without taxes, there wouldn't be towns, cities, civilization! Thoreau wanted to live in a civil community, but without paying to support it. He then addressed me personally, that I ought to pay taxes wherever I settled down. Tomson lectured me, as if he were the pillar of the community. I knew better. He paid the Wilmots bills not for pure charity, with no strings attached, but for the ulterior motive of getting Laura as his reward. Besides, if there in his dirty dossier: the girls he debauched and then left in the streets; those of modest means, who fell behind one or two mortgage payments and his bank quick foreclosure, left them homeless; the business competitors he destroyed, and their employees now on public dole. Add to that, his loudly proclaimed claim of being the exemplary tax-payer, but paying the least by figure manipulation and you dear dad, get the true identity of a corrupt individual, full of foul air. Tomson continued lecturing me that he took me to Walden Pond to learn my lesson of not building a cabin soon, but to building a mansion later, when I had the means to do so. That I shouldn't settle down before the right time. Then, when I had the means to care for myself, I could afford to take care of others by which he meant Laura. The lecture now became a sermon: If I wanted to help the poor, I had first to get rich. He quoted the gospel , that we will always have the poor and I should help them when I was filthy rich, and if I cared. We left Walden Pond, and headed for Cambridge. On that ride back home he tried to influence my politics. That I was going in the wrong direction and go his way, That I should forget the beatniks, the peace-niks and let them break their arses. After all, they were born to end up in the gutter. I thought that with those talents he wanted me to forget Laura, and also to convert me to his politico-economic gospel. When Tomson told me again, to take his loan, to go and see the world and conquer it! I couldn't take it anymore, I asked him to stop the car and let me out. He objected that I'd be at least thirty miles from home. I answered that I could manage to get back home. He stopped the car, but before he let me out he stung me with a poisonous innuendo: that I were putting on an air of sanctity when I wasn't any better than any other full-blooded man. When I asked him to be more explicit, he told me that under the pretence of courting Laura, I was really after her mother-or both. I was shocked to the point that I didn't protest my innocence. He wanted an answer. Whether his allegation were true or not. Assuming that he was right, he inveighed against the old whore who was taking his money but toyed with an insignificant, ugly boy like me. He swore that he'd see to it that I would be sent soon to Vietnam, in order to stop the lurid affair. Then he asked me how I was still around and not in the army, or perhaps I was a draft-dodger already. His allegation that I had an affair with my girl's smother wasn't true as I hadn't done anything

wrong. He was judging my thoughts of which he could have had only a suspicion. Unless he had extracted a confession from her, who knows by what means, of an inconsequential weakness, that, if it had been true, he'd have cared a fig. Finally I had had time to put my thoughts together, and I shouted at him that he was out of his mind and this time he had gone beyond the limits of sanity.

He went off screaming that he would crush me once and forever. I was stunned by the revelation that the widow Cabot's rap was ambiguous toward me. I had no doubt that she really disliked me, as much as I feared her; and yet it seemed that her flesh and mine, had a strange longing for each others. If Tomson had spoken the truth, then her appearances in the living room when she knew that I was there in panties and bra and sometimes in less , might not have been accidental. That my impression that she had squeezed my arm might also have been true. To me all that didn't mean anything. It was an ephemeral frailty that would die out a short while. I still loved Laura more than ever. I still kept wondering if there was a primordial instinct that makes the young get infatuated with the old and vice-versa.

I wondered also, whether it was something that I had inherited from you, dad , knowing of your escapades in up and down directions. Maybe that I was rationalizing my fault making it appear a congenital human one. Then, Tomson had been right, I was not better than he, and as lecherous. As a young man I could fall for mature women, and when I reached his age, I'd fall for adolescent girls. Yet, I rebelled against this kind of determinism. Somehow I was reassured, analyzing my feelings that my love for Laura was intact. That crazy feeling toward her mother, didn't alter a bit

my love for her. She reigned alone over my heart,
my body, and my consciousness. The test result
showed clearly that. I found pleasure watching
her mother's voluptuous body but when she was
out of my sight she was also out of my mind. I
could survive without her but couldn't live without Laura, She was the love of my life. Somebody
said that there is no virtue, where there isn't temp-
tation. Virtue has to prove itself under fire, And
under fire, I resisted, and I presume, she did as
well. Yet, unspoken and unrealized, that sensuous
folly, had debased both of us at least in the critical eye of our consciences, I could have it blotted
out, by it to the human condition an innate part
of the structure of man, saying that it proved that
we were human beings not gods. I also knew that
it was a lie, which having short legs, would have
taken me nowhere. The best thing to do for us,
was to deny our secret longing, whose surrender
would have had the effect of making our mutual
love-hatred more acute, and it would have killed
Laura's love for me. We both did so, without con-
sulting one the other, following this course. I em-
barked on a path of conciliatory behavior toward
the widow Cabot. While I was walking hoping
to hitch-hike my way home, I was reflecting on
Thoreau. His civil disobedience was dear to my
heart. I also thought that his longing for a revival
of the supposed natural state of Man, was naive

at best, his dream of reliving the primitive life in
the wilderness at the location a mile and a half
from the nearest town and civilization; fifty feet
from the railroad tracks: had visible cracks. Anyway, it would have taken a better qualified mind
than the shallow Tomson's to criticize Thoreau.
In the meantime, hundreds of cars had gone by
and none stopped for me. Then a tall, blond mid-
dle-aged gentleman, gave me a ride in a vintage
Buick. I had noticed that it had a bumper-sticker
that read:" Think Tennis." I thought, so what?
He opened up the conversation by saying -dedi-
cation is life's imperative. I thought that I had
encountered one of the Sages of the Land who
had escaped the universal malaise we were in. My
enthusiasm was short-lived. It died the moment
he qualified his thought, and asked me: how did
I think Pancho Segura got to the championship?
-By dedication -I answered him, having gotten
the hint from the bumper-sticker and his motto:
dedication is life's imperative!

When democracy was a political movement in opposition, it had fewer of the blemishes it now exhibits.

—Pareto.

Chapter VII

It was one of those sunny, beautiful spring days that pierce the lingering chill of the dying winter with temperatures above fifty degrees, that the widow Cabot , took her daughter Laura, and Steve's girl friend Amanda to downtown Boston shopping, I' d have liked to go along with them, but I didn't. Steve thought that my idea was crazy. He didn't know that I was used to that kind of shopping. I had tender memories of accompanying my lovely mother on these kinds of adventures. For instance, if she purposely went downtown to buy a pair of shoes chances were pretty high, that she bought a dress, a coat, lingerie, but not shoes. In other words, she had no chartered itinerary. It would have been pretty dull and uneventful if she stopped at a shoe-store, bought a pair of shoes and that was the end of the spree. This kind of predictable future, seemed monotonous to her and to many women, I assume.

The department stores afforded ample possibilities to any adventurous woman. My dear mother, if she was shopping for a hat, why she'd set off with the potentialities of the latest fashion in dresses, their infinite subsections, that showed twists and turns dares and surprises she could touch, feel, try on spoof off? If a woman were courageous, as my mother, she could try on those expensive fur coats that she knew she couldn't ever afford, to see herself in the mirrors pretending to be a duchess, and let her imagination spin. If in the jewelry section, the salesgirl wasn't too busy, she would have a chat with her, while trying on her neck, the most complex designed necklace and liking it, buying a less expensive one, which to her had an unmistakable singularity, and a deep appreciation for the labor of the unknown artist hat she had discovered. We rarely went back home, without taking a look at the sumptuous and delicate furniture, we assumed was bought for being seen, rather than for use. By then, time had run out, and she had to settle for another trip at another time, for buying the item for which he had come, but there was no time for the elaborate selection it required.

To Steve, these forays were odious; to me, they were joyful adventures of a gentle kind. My dear mother was as delicate whether dealing with people or objects. She could see when dealing with workers in their trades, in their faces the unremitting toil they had been through, and treated them with careful understanding. Whatever ob-

ject she didn't care for, she didn't dismiss it completely. She always found in it, that it was at least,
cute or curious. More so with human beings in
distress. Bad as he or she appeared, my mother
always found in them redeeming qualities. If I
have within myself, a tenth of my mother's qualities, I can consider myself a decent human being. Anyway, I stayed with Steve. I had a dish of
vanilla ice cream, and he had a mound of it with
nuts, cherries, and what not. Then he told me
that Tomson was in Washington, and would stay
there for a couple of days as he belonged to the
Council on Foreign Relations, or as it's known,
the invisible government. We laughed, thinking
of what research group this expertise qualified
him for. Then we turned the T.V. on, and soon a
bulletin stopped the regular program. It said that
four students had been killed, and eight others
were wounded, at Kent State University, by the
National Guard. We were shocked. Was that the
ultimate solution, that the Council on National
Defense had stooped to? Was that the easy way
of getting rid of the student protesters? To round
them up on the college campus, as if it were an
ancient Roman arena, and shoot them dead? Cae-
sar and his blood-thirsty cohort in Washington,
will be pleased by the sight of the young victims'
blood. We thought: Are the students in college
the barbarians who pose a threat to the Empire

by pressing near its gates, or are they the martyrs of a democracy fallen into the wrong hands? Or had undue credit been accorded to a concept of a democratic institution that was never realized, and found only in school textbooks for inculcating the catechism of dogmatic politics of this heaven on earth. What we actually have is a majestic Empire. Empires have always been costly. Power and glory are very expensive luxuries, and many things are sacrificed to their altars-The first victim is, of course, the democratic freedom already curtailed by the production system. The Empire to pursue its dream of glory , needs extensive means, which it can acquire, by robbing, either other nations or its own subjects. Look at the other Empires we compete with. The standard of living of their subjects is very low. By and by we will get also to that level. Empire and economic prosperity are often an antithesis. The people have to bear the heavy burden of sustaining armies and costly armaments, by quasi-starvation. Our prosperity will decline as the possibility of exploiting other nations' riches will come to a stop while our dream of glory gets more stubborn, thus drying up more of our national resources. Do we want to be slaves of the Empire, go naked and starving, but basking in its power and glory? Are those the ideals of democracy? The democratic holy writ, beautiful as it is, doesn't match reality. The new renais-

sance found the scholastic texts good, but untrue,
We, of the new generation have a new mode of
perception, which goes beyond the linear, written one. We lifted up our eyes from the written
document, and looked at people, things and insti-
tutions- checking in them, the actual working of
democracy. We found a dramatic gap between the
written word, and the reality, that it was supposed
to have molded. We mentioned the discrepancy
that we saw, and for that reason we have been
persecuted. The news now was really bad: The kids
were shot dead, even though they were unarmed,
and within the college campus. Boys and girls
massacred by a National Guard, while the writ of
democracy was being inculcated to the children
of the victims, brothers and sisters. If tomorrow,
these children will be adults they will find out the
truth about if they have a choice either of loving
it as it is, or leaving it. The third alternative, we
have seen, is that of being shot dead.

While the parents mourn for the death of their
children, the nation ought to mourn for the death
of democracy. The bullets of reality have erased
the last vestiges of its vague appearance, symbol of
veneration of the unknown form of government or
the great lie that we all wanted to believe in wishing it were true. We were warned, and one time
in the past, not to open the jewel-box of faith as
it contained nothing and our discovery would de-

prive the faithful of this crutch, for walking, with their lame understanding through the hard path of life. Now once more, we are warned by people like you and Tomson, that we don't deprive our people, who have already lost the religious faith of this vague dream of democracy: Another pious lie. We say can a lie that kills. Steve, who has a knack for playing the devil's advocate, interjected the official explanation that circumstances killed democracy, and nobody else. It's clear that democracy struggling for survival with oppressive, monolithic states has adopted the enemy's mores. That is our misfortune. Anyway, it's dead.

I wanted to wait for Laura's return, but I had the urge to be alone, to grieve over the bad news, and consider the twist it gave to my future. I had to make a painful decision: whether it was safe for me to stay under the new climate or leave my country. I decided to leave. It was painful. I had to leave behind everything dear to me, a million things that I had taken for granted, at the moment of losing them, become inestimably precious. Most of all ,the house that I have known since I was born, the shell of my dreams. In our mobile age, we still need roots somewhere. Mine are in that white Cape, under the poplar, slender and attractive, that went up straight toward the sky. It was an artistic inspiration in itself. If I close my eyes, I can hear in that house, the echo of my mother's voice. I can also see her moving about it in her diligent care of a child, me, her only child who often fell asleep, exhausted by dreaming of distant Lands that he envisioned full of the ruins of their past splendor. He saw them loaded with history and got there coming down majestic rivers whose banks had infinite lines of poplars, just like the one by his house that added a touch of distinction to those enchanted places. That single poplar, in my dream propagated in every land that I visited. It evoked the fabulous places while entrancing me, rustling when the big Nor-easter whipped it mercilessly, while I laid on my back on a mat by the closed back door, in the semi-darkness of the basement. What most troubled me was if I left the country, what would Laura do? Would she come with me? Her decision was much more painful to make than mine. I wished with all my heart, that we'd be together in any place on earth. First I had to tell you, dear dad, of my decision to leave the country. I don't have to tell you what happened, I was lucky to get out of the house alive. You saw it as a personal offense to you, You, dear dad, called me a traitor, imbecile, gutless, the unbearable cross of your life. We parted both broken-hearted. My calvary had just begun. I had two more slippery posts to climb: Laura and her mother. I took Laura to dinner at Stouffers, at the Prudential tower. After dinner, we walked along the bank of the Charles River. We walked, stopped, threw some pebbles in the water, walked some more, without saying a word. Then abruptly with my heart pumping fast, I squeezed her to my chest, and told her that I had to leave for Canada in three days time; that I couldn't leave or live without her. We had a good cry in each other's arms. Laura told me, not only that she would come with me, but also, for the first time ever, that she loved me. That was all I wanted to hear. At that moment I felt really happy. If the entire world were to turn against me, it would not conquer me with Laura at my side. Actually I had wished for an easier course of events, as I was now more attached to life than ever, but what about her mother and brother? I've always felt empathy for other people's sorrows and now I was going to cause some good amount of it myself, I took Laura home wishing to find her mother and Steve there. My great hope was that they would give us their blessings. They became crimson with emotion, I told both how I had never deliberately injured anyone. I tried putting things in perspective that in fact we were all victims of circumstances, which none of us had created. I didn't make a dent in Agatha Cabot's disapproval. She loved her daughter and in her consuming pride, wanted to see her on the pinnacle of what to her was success: money and a position in the best society. Looking down on me, the duchess addressed me as if I were a servant aspiring to a higher rank, that I wasn't the right man to give her daughter what she deserved. In her estimation, it was her daughter's status that mattered. As she had chosen the non exalted one whether she would be living faraway in Canada or next door, was irrelevant. To her, Laura's decision showed coarse taste and blindness, faults that she had inherited from her father's side, of course. She was certain that with me, Laura wouldn't ever enter the earthly paradise, that is, her mother's circle. Turning to me, in her eyes, was worthless. I had shown my colors by shirking from my duty toward our beloved and glorious country. By this idiosyncracy I had made manifest my weak-spined ancestors. She slightly knew me but inferred that all my ancestors from way back, had betrayed the king first and then the republic. They all had been like me, scrawny rascals, who had never stood for honor, devotion, ideals, and nothing could ever raise them up to the level of patriots.

She displayed all the wisdom made up of cliches so comfortable to the distracted and the indifferent. Should I have retorted that she was wrong? From where should I have begun? In order to make her understand what I stood for, I should have had to reconstruct her entire life.

Confronted by the impossible, I left her with her cliches. Did my mother think along the same lines as the widow Cabot, and had she wanted me to climb the highest peaks? Of course she did. You also, dear dad, wanted to see me a hero in uniform, a terror to the entire world and a conqueror of it. On the other hand my mother spurred me toward a place in our culture, trying to ascend to its throne done without shedding blood, without stepping on heaps of human bones. That's the realm of the arts where excellence doesn't destroy nor compromise human dignity.

Dear dad, don't be hasty to curse the memory of my dear mother for the direction and development of my life. She inspired me, but the bulk of responsibility for what I have become rests on my shoulders . I was born with the tendency toward the pacific life. I have always watched the world with a benign eye, and my effort has always aimed at reducing its thorns. I have always felt pain watching a felled tree or cruelty toward an animal. Most of all, I'm appalled at the evil perpetrated by human beings on other human beings. Yes, dear dad, this is the son of yours that has gone astray. You still don't think of me as a well rounded man. I lack the attributes that in your eyes, makes the he-man. Today, without taking much pride in it, and without false humility, I tell you that I am a man whatever judgment is passed on me by anyone. Whether you, dear dad, love or hate me, I'm still your son.

Going back to the widow Cabot, I,'ve tried to see if I could find any resemblance of outlook on life, between her and my mother's. They had in common a distinction of manners, and a touch sf elegance that appeal to any man of cultivated taste. By the way, my mother's lineage wasn't so coarse as the widow Cabot had inferred. It was at least, as distinct as the widow Cabot's. Those and no others were the three things they had in common. For the rest of their qualities, they were miles apart. My mother, for instance, if she had had a daughter, wouldn't have tried to sacrifice her for riches and status. At that moment I was facing a mother whose pride had blinded her maternal love. When her language got unbearable I was going to leave but she couldn't miss the pleasure of throwing me out. Before I opened the door, she ordered me to get out of her house. Before leaving I glanced at my dear Laura. From her expression I knew that she was on my side. Steve caught me in the vestibule, and putting his hand on my shoulder, extracted from me the promise that I'd care for the well-being of his sister. I asked him to throw some distortion an the right date of our departure, just in case Tomson along with his connections, tried stopping us. Steve added in a somber tone, that his mother and himself, would miss Laura terribly. I understood perfectly their feelings. In a consoling gesture, I embraced him dearly. I also knew that Laura would painfully miss her mother and her brother. I couldn't refrain myself from blaming Tomson for my predicament. If he hadn't used his connections, I perhaps wouldn't have been drafted, and wouldn't have to leave the country. Any remedy to that was now impossible.

We left our country either for a while or forever. Dear dad, you have to believe me that it was painful for me to tear Laura from her family. Since then years have gone by and I still don't know, and perhaps never will, what mother and daughter said to one another after I left their home. I only know, that my mother-in-law, like you, dad, has never come to see us and never answered our letters. Now let me relate, dear dad, an episode in my life that confirms the low esteem you have of me-That happened a few days before our departure. First of all why did I choose Montreal, you'd ask? Because it's easier to get here from our native town in Massachusetts, and not because Laura and I were fluent in French. Anyway, as we needed money to live north of the border and I had the responsibility of taking care not only of myself but also of my dear Laura, although she wasn't helpless ,and working together, we'd make it here or anywhere else. I'd have preferred to move to Italy, the land of the arts, but we couldn't at all afford to do so, besides, if we knew very little French, the only Italian we knew was pizza. The problem for me was where to get the money that we needed to go north. As you, dear dad, told me that you would not give me a dime, I closed my savings account, which amount came close to paying for a tankful of gas for my Chevy. I was compelled to sell a few things. I sold most of my mother's jewelry, but I kept one of her rings that I meant to put on Laura's finger the day we could afford to get married. I sold the Britannica, and most of my books except The Federalist Papers, The Revolt of The Masses, two French novels: Rouge et Noir and La Chartreuse de Parme, and an English French dictionary. We knew that in Montreal they speak English besides French, but we wanted to learn the local idiom and hoped to be making many French friends. I thought it was my duty to go and say good-bye to uncle Ed, who had always been good to me.

My mother's brother gave me what sum of money he could, perhaps at his I income a large family deprivation, but best of all his blessing. I had a problem with Laura's sudden joyful atti-tude, as if, on the verge to going into exile, she were leaving on a cruise. She went to every party she was invited to in her finery- At first I was pleased to hear her laughter, while dancing with every young man she knew from school, or a distant relative of hers.

At the third party, I grew a bit jealous, also afraid, whether she had changed her mind about following me in exile or was keeping her promise. From my attitude she realized that I was unhappy with her behavior and she put my fears to rest, telling me that she loved me, and only me and had also already packed her belongings. At that moment scales fell off my eyes,

that till then dimmed, had let her appear to me a Sphinx. I realized that she wasn't an enigma. Sphinxes don't really love, don't make sacrifices, don't take sides, don't comfort, don't watch after you and don't stand beside you when nobody else does. We have shared our sorrows as well our moments of happiness. I have to tell you, dear dad, that she's been a blessing to me. Have I like-wise been a blessing to her? It's not for me to say. I only am certain, that without Laura, I'd have thrown myself to the wind. With her declaration of love for me, not only she dispelled my jealousy , but also, the reason for her frolicking at those parties, even with Tomson. With it she was throwing a screen to hide our scheme from everybody, especially from Tomson. With her feminine charm, she was trying to appease the monster, that salivated to devour her and knowing that soon she was going to leave her mother and brother hostages in his hands, Laura also,

used those occasions as her hast opportunities to mingle with her cousins, friends, schoolmates. Behind she was leaving a world dear to her, that soon she knew to say good-bye to , perhaps forever.

It is our task to plant trees
which may be of value
for another age.

—Grotius

Chapter VIII

The time of departure had arrived. First we went to shed our tears on her father's grave, and then at my mother's. I wanted to say good-bye to you, dear dad, but you couldn't be found., I called you on the phone, but there was no answer. I didn't want to leave you all alone, but I had to leave. We packed our few belongings in the trunk of my old Chevy and drove North, toward our uncertain future, Laura and I, and a few young people in the same predicament and resolution renewed the wandering of our ancestors, the Pilgrims who fled England because its institutions were hostile to the dictates of their conscience, We, likewise, fled from our land and heritage, as mutations in institutions and policies created an atmosphere that was hostile to our consciences, We can't live in retrospective dreams of the past, and yet we wondered if the Pilgrims and the Revolutionary founders of our country foresaw that their labors and hopes, would end up like this. Their immeasurable sacrifices were all in vain. An immense and powerful Empire stands majestically whereas quality of life was sought and sowed. On the other hand, we, new Pilgrims of civilization, haven't the least illusion of a new beginning. We fled to a country that can do the least evil. No more than that.

The first day we arrived in Montreal, with our two suitcases and our small amount of money, we rested in Christ Church. There was only a young man lying on its front lawn. Inside there was nobody. Sitting in one of its empty pews we thought what to do, in total quietness. Why did we rest in a church, as soon we were in another country, immigrants without a friend there to welcome us? Both of us thought ourselves as being unbelievers. We hadn't put a foot in a church in a long time, and chided our friends who still did. At the time, I hadn't succeeded in severing my belief completely as I had still doubt about the afterlife, and it ravaged my intellectual fabric and my actions. Laura was also not entirely free. While she abjured any transcendental nonsense, I came to know, that one night, during the rehearsal of her last

High-School play she was at the vestry of the Congregational Church, she went upstairs and thinking she was alone, and knelt down and sobbed in the dark. Remembering that episode, I put my arm over her shoulders and asked her as we were going to live together, if she wanted to marry me. The promise to live for one another was there but marriage was telling the world that our bond was public. We agreed on getting married. Soon after we looked at the church's stained glass windows, and realized that, we who had fled from military coercion, had paused in a church dedicated to the God of Hosts. Beneath those powerful pine-beams you could read pages of British dominion over this land. It reminded us of the King's Chapel in Boston. There the history of the English rule over the American Colonies is forever told by the private stall of the Viceroy and of other high-rank officials. Here, in Christ Church, the history of dominion, is told by the stained-glass windows, donated in memory of the British generals and other military ranks. They tell silently of British garrisons that kept dominion over this French population. The long list of the church's ministers, tell the same oppressive story. All its ministers served a two year term. When he term expired, they returned to their homeland. We expected, if he came the actual minister would be British. We weren't disappointed. The Rev. Meredith was an English looking man ,a tall, blond, jovial fellow, in his early thirties. Thank goodness, he wasn't martial at all. We liked him and he us. Besides the instant bond of friendship, we had the other of being strangers in this land. We asked Rev. Meredith to marry us. It was done in a simple ceremony. He was of much help to us. First of all, he helped us find an apartment to live in. Next I had to find a job and soon; before running out of our small amount of money. After knocking, in vain on this and that door, I found a job as a truck-driver. At first we had a hard life, but we survived. Many other refugees weren't so lucky. As their little money dwindled, their standard of living followed suit. Two meals a day and a room in a cold flat, were soon reduced to one frugal meal a day, and a corner of a basement, for passing the cold nights in. When they ran out of money and jobs were not in sight, it was for them either begging or starving, and sleeping in doorways. In the bitter cold of winter, they ran out of warm clothes and footwear. Then they vanished from the face of the earth unnoticed by anyone, as their ancestors, who didn't survive the privations and the harsh winter of 1620 at the Plymouth Plantation, our dear friends perished in this cold land, where we all came to find refuge. Meanwhile, on the other side of the border, young men kept coming home in coffins wrapped in Old Glory, and being buried with pomp and gun-salute, fine example of the "dulce et decorum est pro patria mori". The young men who died here had no decent burial, weren't wrapped in flags, no tears were shed over them. Today I spread over them, the invisible flag of humanity, under whose colors they struggled and died. History will not forget their pacific uprising. It tallies higher than the shot heard around the world, as a sublime act on the positive side of civilization. Laura and I helped the few we could. It didn't amount to real help, as at the times we ourselves, were hanging precariously on the survival level. Now that I own the trucking business, that I used to work for I employ quite a few of my fellow-refugees. Our door has always been open to those in need, be they friend or foe. Anyway I don't do much claim for the little good that we have done. Chances are that we have received much, and have given little in return.

Dear dad , I want you to know, that I have been fulfilling my mother' wish through thick and thin, I haven't neglected my studies. I attended evening classes at Mc Gill-Today I got my Master's degree. And yet, I'm still intellectually not satisfied, looking for better knowledge that will make me wiser, more humane as the years go by. The reason why we should know more is that with it we can improve ourselves and others and by doing so we all get more civilized day by day. I also hope that before returning to dust, I as one of the chorus, will come to understand more of the universal drama. I am not longing for eternal peace, or absolute redemption that transcends life, rather for peace among men that will let them fulfill their destiny on earth, and afford them a look into the "streaming horizons of geological and stellar histories". Laura also goes nights to McGill, enrolled at the Ecole des Beaux Arts. Given her devotion to the arts we have a plan to go to Italy, some time in the future for her development in painting and sculpture. She's already sold some works in both canvas and marble. You, dear dad, should come and see with your own eyes, what an accomplished artist she has become! When will that day be? Whenever you decide, we will always welcome you.

Going back to Laura, she could go to night-classes because we alternated baby- sitting for our baby daughter Sophia. Our love was crowned by her arrival. At Sophia's birth, when I went into the new-babies' ward, and saw her for the first time, although it was against regulation, I twisted the nurse's arm to let me touch her with one finger, my newborn baby. Touching her, I made the wish for her for a long and happy life. That wish grew into a prayer. It surrounds her night and day. As I couldn't be with her every moment , I'm always with her in thought. If she could see through thin air she'd see me watching her. Were it in my power, I'd have made her a goddess; but being what I am, I can only give her my infinite love, and my best wishes for a full life, and the best of everything it can offer. It's obvious that I've tried passing on to her, the love and care that my mother gave me. Anyway, what I want to tell you, dear dad, is that if you ever get tired of flying for any other reason, want a change of pace, come up here. As a newborn baby, you welcomed me in your house, and made it mine. Now I own a house, which in turn is also your house. If you come, and you like it you can be president of my modest enterprise or whatever it pleases you to be. Come and join us, your family, at any time! Last summer, after years of silence, my brother-in-law Steve carne to see us. He teaches Math now at Cambridge High, and he's married to Amanda the red-haired daughter of T.S. Buckley, the Harvard administrator. He's being groomed for a position at the University. Knowing what kind of a person Steve is, I'm sure that Harvard has nothing to lose, and much to gain, if that transaction will take place. Steve's not only a competent but a brilliant scholar. On the occasion he took Amanda to the international exposition in the summer of 1970, " Terre des Hommes" was still being held here in Montreal. He sneaked out of her sight or under other pretext as Amanda, he thought would tell his mother on him. He and Laura embraced dearly. Tears streaked down his cheeks when he took our little Sophia in his arms. Laura glanced at me inquiring whether it was right asking about her mother. I nodded my assent.

I'd have asked about my mother- in-law myself but thought it was proper if done by her daughter. Laura asked Steve, how her mother was doing. Steve answered that their mother was doing and feeling well. She was a bit heavier now, but still lively as ever, that money and luxuries remained the goals in the horizon of her life. Then he confided to his sister, that their mother did miss her daughter a lot at first then adjusted to the new situation well. He checked the time on his wristwatch, and said apprehensively that he must leave. He kissed his sister and our Sophia lingering his hands around their one normal and the other tiny waists lingering his hands as an effort of taking a part of them with him, and headed for the door. I stopped him and asked if Tomson was still around. Steven answer was that the old Minotaur was still around, but so decrepit, that I wouldn't recognize him, and yet more pathetic. He now kept hanging around Middle Schools. High-School girls are too old for him. Steve added that a little more of Tomson's reckless life, and his mother might get his money after all. We watched him from the doorstep, till he vanished around the corner. I kept wondering on Tomson's and my mother-in-law's quality of life. They thought that the gallant life was the epitome of the whole of life: as opposed to the provincial life, which was relegated to a remote and obscure corner of it. They missed perceiving their own provinciality when they mistake the socialite's life, often so shallow, that has to be sustained continuously oiled and outfitted with props of distraction to avoid the crushing ennui for the whole of life and what it is. The Dionysian side of life has its right of being explored and enjoyed, not exclusively but in harmony with the other sides of life. As for me I live and let live.

Au crepuscule des mes jours
Rejoignez, s'il se peut, l'aurore.

—Voltaire

Chapter IX

Dear dad, I've come to the end of the synopsis of events, feeling and thoughts that informed what to you has been, my reprobate action. I touched upon politics, as I saw it affecting my life in its vast assumption of an imperial nature, but couched in the terms of meek and friendly aspirations of a democratic nation. I mentioned ethics, as the foundation of private and public behavior; the path on which everyone should confidently walk, rather than the one of arrogance of power disguised as moral commitments. With those lies, we further our ambitions, which we are unable to renounce or even to curtail, thus spelling more future confrontations, paid by the sacrifice of many lives. I also expressed my personal feelings: all that, in order to make you, dear dad, understand why I did what I did. It's also important to me to answer your question about who and what I am. From the few things that I have mentioned, for they are an infinitesimal part of my thoughts and feelings and therefore could never make an accurate portrayal of me, did I make a distinct sketch of a good man or of a monster? I could not ever be a monster, because I'd rather be the victim than the killer; better yet, neither. I've always wanted to be good and live among good people-It's simply a wish that seems impossible to have come true. Perhaps it's best to remain such. I feared, that a world where every human being were good, the world would prove to be too monotonous, and too sugary to bear.

Is this tenet in praise of evil acceptable? I disagree. The world does not need much more evil than it already has. Is it not, in its natural aspects, already replete with the evil of sickness, suffering and death? Life's seasoned with evil and doesn't need the added evil made by man. Who does need the latter addition to make life in this world perfectly imperfect? Of course we don't! I know for sure, that we don't need evil human beings to season with their venom, the good people's lives to make it bearable. If now that turmoil, hatred, murder, are so wide spread, choking off infinitesimal good, yet we go on living. Wouldn't an overwhelming good, make a better world, where we all were breathing in an atmosphere mostly good, with mischief lost in tiny foul air pockets? As for me:-let me live in a world of good, seasoned with a dash of inevitable evil rather than in a world full of evil, and only a scent of good. Am I a dreamer? If so, what possible evil can come from dreaming good dreams beneficent to mankind? Otherwise are the good precepts that we have learned at our mothers' knees, to be forgotten? Is the civilization that upholds them a screen hiding the eternal jungle rather than a means to transform and redeem it? I don't intend to waste my life arguing over it. I concentrate on living my life. Dear dad, all these years I've written many letters to you and I've never gotten any answers. I know that the CIA opens my mail, but I think that you have received it. Read this synopsis, and answer me, please?

Your son, who will always love you,
Buzz -That's my nickname you called me.

Dear dad, I was going to send you the synopsis of my life as a a gesture sf reconciliation between us. Now there is no reason to do so. Uncle Ed informed me that you are no more. I'm sorry that I couldn't be at your funeral. I'm on my own now. For many years I've thought of what it means, being a man. Now, having lost the remotest hope of relying on anyone else, I'm a real man. In the past I thought that when my day came, I'd be interred between my mother's grave and yours. That simple wish has become impossible to come true. When my time comes, I will buried ,who knows where. And yet, the destiny of man is that of returning to dust forever, will it matter where one

will be buried? It shouldn't. Is this another piece
of provinciality, still lingering on even among the
best of us. We also should get rid of it, as we have
done with the bond with the ethnic groups we belong to, to the nationality, the religions , even the
family we were born in. Only when we succeed
in getting rid of prejudices, can we call ourselves
civilized human beings. Am I civilized? Were you
civilized? Why on earth do I keep I talking to
you, dear dad, knowing that you aren't here anymore? Because I have a few things to get off my
chest that I did not had a chance to discuss with
you. Before we parted, I had always asked your
opinion on what I planned to do. I wanted your
opinion and most of all your approval. I needed
it. Just by asking for your opinion it was a relief
to me, I had grown so used to your disapproval,
that it meant to me whatever I did we did it together. Does it make sense? Now I've to make,
without your disapproval, quick decisions, guided
by the cardinal points of reference of conscience,
my consciousness, and a bit of intuition. Have I
chosen the best way to spend my life? By accept-
ing life as it as bestowed on us by destiny, and
the human environment, upon both we had no
say in it: drifting down its mighty current is living of a kind. If one can steer life's course , away
from rocks, waterfalls, man-made dams that arrest and sometimes destroy its natural flow, for

the benefit of no one, but for increasing the foolish pride of rulers, in my opinion this is living the civilized life. Living is loving life. Because the personal course life takes for each one of us is unknown it shouldn't have any omissions, any regrets, any postponement of action that the moment demands of us, lest tomorrow be too late, as the course itself might have ended. Shirking from our responsibilities will result in mutilation of our life without a second chance ever.

Dear dad, I wish that you lived your life as you saw it best without any regrets. All these years I've waited for the proper time to ask you a very important question, which now will never be answered. If I had had the opportunity to have asked you, in the most delicate way, if ever there was a delicate way handling ethical matters that stand formidable and immobile within the majestic realm of human achievements. Has your conscience ever bothered you for having killed with smart-bombs, napalm, and the like in the service of your country, of course, so many human beings? My wish is that you had remorse. Regret for one's evil doing is a humane sign, an admission of guilt, of having a conscience to reckon with. The human beast, on the other hand, has no regrets as he hasn't reached the level of knowing and choosing between right and wrong, good and evil. Was I, in your eyes, with my conscientious objection to war, a living reproach before the bar of your conscience, pointing at what you yourself should have done rather than joining the murderers' ranks? That would explain your unforgiving attitude towards me. You'd have liked to see me among the killers, but because I didn't, you hated me like everyone who behaved like me. If I had become a murderer like every one in your ranks, I could not point a finger accusing anyone of them as I were one of the conscienceless jungle-beasts. Did you, dear dad, believe in God?

If you did, you knew that there was no forgiveness for the evil that you perpetrated on your fellow men. If you didn't believe in God, then you rejoiced in his absence. While you delighted in His absence, I mourned it. Not because it let you go scot free. But because it has let loose the hordes of criminals which belief in God's existence had kept somewhat in check kept their criminal impulses. And yet, beyond the vision of God, can anyone who has within himself the vision of mankind's brotherhood harm anyone? My answer, and everyone else's ought to be, No.

Epilogue

Johann C.F. Schiller's" Ode an die Freude", that someday, all men will be brothers set in music by Ludwig von Beethoven in his 9th Symphony tells their aspiration for world peace. They aren't the only two in history to have wished for a universal peace. Just on what I can remember at this moment, we can include Euripides, Lucretius, Saint Francis of Assisi, and of course Schiller and Beethoven, in the tiny group. Millennia have passed waiting for that day of world peace. Will that day ever come? The world is still divided into many nation states; the large and Strong ones trying to dominate the small and weak ones. Even the landing of man on the moon and the picture that Neil Armstrong took from there, that showed our planet Earth, small ,and lost in the immensity of the Universe, we still can't see that we are here together, not as many nations but as the inhabitants of this speck of dust. Our provincial outlook hasn't been dislodged by the vision of our planet seen from outer space. The earthlings are still fighting among themselves, as if they were enemies rather than brothers. Do we have a world flag? We still have our many provincial flags. Didn't Armstrong, the astronaut who first landed on the moon, while declaring that his was a small step for a man, but a big one for mankind, plant there our United States flag? Shouldn't the message have been that the earth's inhabitants had reached the moon? No. It was the Americans that had accomplished that feat.

Will ever the day come when we are singing the Ode an die Feude not only with our mouths but also with our hearts: Interim, shouldn't we hoist the Olympic flag that's more international than our provincial ones? We should. While wait ing for the world to unify in peace, I go on liv ing the best way I can. As a matter sf fact, now that we can afford to go to Europe, we'll soon go there for a while. Laura wants to stay there mainly in Italy, to perfect her craft. Her long ing for Italy could be an ancestral calling, given that the Cabots a long time ago, originated from Italy. Of course she isn't totally Italian. She is a melange of Italian, English, French, with a dash of German, and a smidgen of American Indian. Thinking of it, aren't we all a melange of a num ber of so called nationalities? I'm as far as I know, a complex of Scottish, French, Russian and a dash of American Indian. What is the compound that our daughter Sophia's made of? Add my ancestry to Laura's, plus that she's Canadian born, and what do we have? A Canadian citizen. We are all full of prejudices. The land that we or our ancestors came from, has been given different names but we all are sons and daughters of the planet earth. Somebody reminded us that the surface of the globe that we call land is or was one. Let's see, Europe is a peninsula of Asia. Asia, before the Suez Canal was dug was attached to Africa. The American continent wasn't divided by the Bering strait from Asia, it tied them. The Australian continent, was attached by what are now innumerable islands in a chain, to Asia.. Ergo, the land surface of the earth is one, and its population is also one. Going back to our plans, Laura has a mind to spend days, if not months in Florence, Rome, Venice and Naples; to visit all the museums and art galleries there, and come back to Montreal, only when we run out of money. Next year if we can afford it, we'll go to Paris, Versailles, Fontainebleau. After spending a long time in the Louvre, the Musee des Arts Decoratif, we'll descend to Provence. The years after we'll visit Dresden, Vienna, Saint Petersburg, and London. We'll visit the sights, museums, galleries, but we'll mingle with the local people wherever we go. We 'll come back home with wider horizons, more civilized, more cultured, more of world citizens. However, the three of us can't make the world one nor the people in it one. Let us all unite and sing the Ode an die Freude, not only with our mouths but also with our hearts!

Printed in the United States
201853BV00001B/1-105/A

9 781587 369155